WELCOME!

THIS BOOK BELONGS TO:

_____

_____

It all started with a small, yellow cell and over Minions . . . wait, millions of years, the Minions evolved.

Each Minion is different, but they all share the same goal - to find and serve the most despicable master possible.

As Minion history tells us, finding a master was easy. Keeping a master alive was the hard part. From the biggest and bossiest singled-celled amoeba, to an evil amphibian that the Minions followed out of the sea, to early mankind, the Minions have lost their employers in a variety of ways.

In this book, you can learn all about the Minions' journey and fill in the book with your own details, secrets and favourite things!

ALL ABOUT ME!

MY NAME IS _____

MY BIRTHDAY IS _____

I AM _____ years old

I WAS BORN IN _____

MY HAIR COLOUR IS _____

MY EYE COLOUR IS _____

MY HEIGHT IS _____

MY SHOE SIZE IS _____

MY FAVOURITE FRUIT IS (banana, obviously)

_____

MY DREAM JOB IS _____

KT-116-508

Draw yourself
in the box below:

It's time to brush up on your Minions knowledge – how much do you know about them?

WHO ARE THE MINIONS?

The Minions are a tribe of loveable, but accident-prone little yellow creatures. They love their Minion brothers, serving the biggest, baddest villain they can find, and bananas!

WHAT DO THEY LOOK LIKE?

- Yellow
- Goggles
- One or two eyes
- **Super-cool outfits** *(these vary depending on the era, but are always awesome!)*

FAVOURITE THINGS:

Bananas, their buddies, evil plans, making mischief

KEY PHRASES IN 'MINION':

"Blumock"

"Bello!"

"Big Boss!"

IF YOU EVER SEE A MINION . . .

DO:
- **Give them a banana** *(is there any better way to make friends?)*
- **Something funny**
- **Laugh**
- **Respect the goggles**

DON'T:
- **Come between a Minion and their banana**
- **Get in the way of an evil plan**
- **Think they're all the same; each Minion is brilliant in their own special way**

If you're in need of a plan or a Minion of action –
Kevin is the one you want.

ALIASES: Kevin, Kev-bo, Seventh Kevin, Sir Kevin

KEVIN IS . . . proud, clever, "big brother", not so
great at public speaking

BEST MOMENTS:

The discovery of the Minions' blue overalls

Playing polo while riding a corgi

Finding Scarlet Overkill

[Add your favourite Kevin moment here:]

_____

_____

_____

_____

_____

DISLIKES:
Disappointing
his Big
Boss

LIKES:
Protecting his buddies,
spending time with
Bob and Stuart, Lava
Guns, epic adventures,
flying in Scarlet's jet,
heists, Villain-Con,
police chases, the
Nelson family

Draw a line of Minions following Kevin to find a
new master.

ALL ABOUT STUART!

Musician. Lover. Hungry. These are three words that describe Stuart – there are probably more, but we don't have a dictionary to hand.

NAME: Stuart, Stu, Stu-art, Stu-perman, Beef Stu

STUART IS . . . cool, musical, flirt, always hungry

BEST MOMENTS:

Sleeping through Kevin's speech and accidentally volunteering for the mission

Falling in love with a yellow fire hydrant

Relaxing in the hot tub in his thong bikini

Rocking out in front of Buckingham Palace

[Add your favourite Stuart moment here:]

_____

_____

_____

_____

_____

_____

LIKES: Playing his ukulele, hot tub

DISLIKES: Snow globes

12

ROCK AND ROLL

Draw Stuart rocking out on stage.

Bob is the smallest Minion. However, what he lacks in size he makes up for in heart.

NAME: Bob, Robert, Bobby, My Boy, "King Bob"

BOB IS . . . Overly excited, sweet, lovable, "little brother"

BEST MOMENTS:

Making Tim dance when asked if he has any evil talents, at the Henchmen Placement Specialist Stand

Swallowing the red ruby

Pulling the sword from the stone

Giving his speech as King

[Add your favourite Bob moment here:]

_____

_____

_____

_____

_____

_____

LIKES:
His teddy bear Tim, giggling, playing hide and seek, making friends

DISLIKES:
Bees, being away from his buddies, losing Tim

A FEW OF BOB'S
FAVOURITE THINGS!

Draw and colour things you think Bob
might like on this page.

HOW TO BE A MINION

It's time to learn to release your inner Minion!

There's much more to being a Minion than being yellow. Here are some things to follow to help you bring out your inner Minion.

Follow these simple guides to discover your inner Minion. Bananas are not optional.

- **A key part of being a Minion is a love of bananas They're yellow, sweet and delicious!**
- **Serving your master in the best way you can is also important.**
- **Developing and testing new weapons: you've got to know they'll work before you give them to your master.**
- **Laugh and be excited: is there anything better than helping your master be evil? (No, the answer is no!)**
- **In life and everything, be the best you can be!**
- **Good goggle care – it's vital to be able to see when you live in a big tribe and there are lots of things to trip over!**
- **Have we mentioned bananas? Yes? Well, we can't express how much Minions love bananas.**
- **If there is some music playing, you *must* dance.**
- **Be ready for anything and everything at every possible moment!**

MINIONS, MINIONS EVERYWHERE!

You can never have too many Minions!
How many Minions can you count on these pages?

THERE ARE _____ MINIONS.

HOW MANY
MINIONS
WITH ONE
EYE CAN YOU
COUNT?

HOW DID YOU DO?
Check your answers
on page 94.

23

Take this quiz to find out!

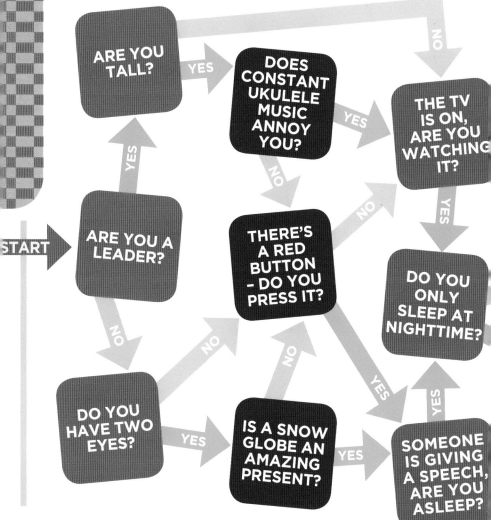

START

ARE YOU A LEADER?

YES → ARE YOU TALL?

YES → DOES CONSTANT UKULELE MUSIC ANNOY YOU?

YES → THE TV IS ON, ARE YOU WATCHING IT?

NO

NO → THERE'S A RED BUTTON – DO YOU PRESS IT?

NO

THE TV IS ON, ARE YOU WATCHING IT?

YES → DO YOU ONLY SLEEP AT NIGHTTIME?

NO → DO YOU HAVE TWO EYES?

YES → IS A SNOW GLOBE AN AMAZING PRESENT?

YES → SOMEONE IS GIVING A SPEECH, ARE YOU ASLEEP?

YES

YES

DO YOU THINK TIE-DYE SHIRTS LOOK COOL?

NO →

DO YOU ALWAYS HAVE A PLAN?

YES →

YES ↓

WOULD YOU BE THE LEAD SINGER IN A BAND?

YES →

DO YOU LOVE THE UKULELE?

YES →

NO

NO

KEVIN

YES →

IF A SONG IS PLAYING, DO YOU SING ALONG?

YES →

IS A LUNCHBOX THE BEST WAY TO CARRY A TEDDY AROUND?

YES →

NO

STUART

NO

BOB

BEST FRIENDS FOREVER!

The Minions might squabble sometimes . . . and fight sometimes, but they're the best of friends. Draw yourself with your best friends below.

GADGETS

An important part of being a Minion is supplying your master with gadgets for their evil doings. Here are some examples of the best gadgets.

CLUB: Simple. Effective. Many consider this to be the original gadget, others argue that the stick was first and this is just larger. Whichever you believe, when the Minions armed Caveman with this gadget, he became a formidable evil force.

FLY SWATTER: A fantastic gadget if your master is waging a war against flies. It is not so good if your master is battling with a bear. The result is delicious for the bear ONLY.

SWORD: Or 'cutlass' in more piratey terms. Great for ruling the seven seas, waving menacingly at sharks or other enemies and for cutting food.

CANNON: These make an impressive and exciting BOOM and can shoot cannon balls at approaching armies. Always make sure they're not aimed at your boss.

What sort of gadget would you give your master to use?
DRAW IT BELOW.

NAME: _____

USES OF MY GADGET: _____

HERB OVERKILL. Now there was someone who could design a CRAZY gadget. Turn to page 74 to find out more!

MINION NAME GENERATOR

You might call them Minions, but actually each Minion goes by their own name. Use this handy tool to find your Minion name.

Write your human name here: _____

Write it backwards (just for fun!): _____

Which month were you born in?_____

Match your birth month to your new Minion name below.

JANUARY	STUART	JULY	BRIAN
FEBRUARY	BOB	AUGUST	NORBERT
MARCH	KEVIN	SEPTEMBER	HENRY
APRIL	DAVE	OCTOBER	JERRY
MAY	MIKE	NOVEMBER	CARL
JUNE	CHRIS	DECEMBER	TOM

30

Write your Minion name here, so you don't forget.

Hello
my name is

MY FAMILY TREE

The Minion tribe is like a family because they're all created from the same strand of DNA – sort of like you and your family (without getting too sciencey!) Fill in your family tree onto this page!

Photo

MY SIBLING'S NAME
_____

YOUR NAME
_____

A photo of me

Photo

MY SIBLING'S NAME
_____

MY SIBLING'S NAME
_____

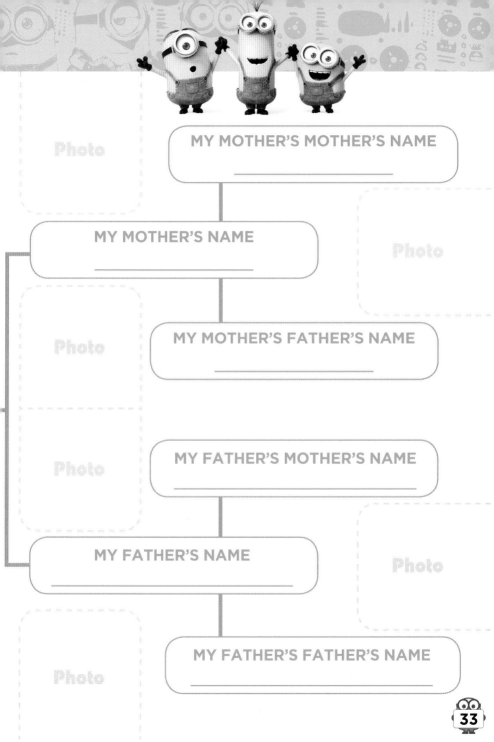

Photo

MY MOTHER'S MOTHER'S NAME

_____

MY MOTHER'S NAME

_____

Photo

Photo

MY MOTHER'S FATHER'S NAME

_____

Photo

MY FATHER'S MOTHER'S NAME

_____

MY FATHER'S NAME

_____

Photo

Photo

MY FATHER'S FATHER'S NAME

_____

Dinosaur Era Fact File

MASTER: T. REX

When the Minions followed their evil amphibian master out of the sea onto the land, their master was crushed by something larger and more evil . . . a Tyrannosaurus rex!

They'd found their new master!

FACT FILE

NAME: Tyrannosaurus rex (it means 'Tyrant Lizard' – how evil is that!)

TIME PERIOD: Late Cretaceous period (65–70 million years ago . . . WOW, that's a long time ago!)

BEST MASTER TRAITS:

Terrifying roar

Long, sharp teeth

Large enough to carry up to 20 Minions at a time

EVIL RATING: 6 out of 10 skulls

FAVOURITE MEMORIES:

How the Minions lost the T. rex as their master:

The lure of a bunch of bananas was too much to resist . . . even if they're under a large rock. The rock started rolling, pushing the T. rex into a volcano. Oops!

Dino Close-Up

The Minions are so enamoured with their master that they sometimes get too close.

Can you spot these close-up images in the larger pictur

1

2

3

4

PLEASE BE WARNE
NEVER GET THIS CLOSE TO
T. REX IF YOU'RE ATTACHE
TO ALL OF YOUR LIMBS
(and wish to remain so).

36

HOW DID YOU DO?
Check your answers on page 94.

37

Making an outfit from leaves

In many ways, prehistory was a simpler time. In other ways, the Minions had to make clothes from whatever they could find.

Can you dress these two Minions using things you can find in your garden? Use glue to stick your outfit down.

CAVEMAN ERA
FACT FILE

Man was very different to dinosaurs. Shorter, hairier and WAY smarter. The Minions took an instant liking to man, even though they weren't always the smartest species around . . .

FACT FILE

NAME: Caveman

TIME PERIOD: 10,000 years ago

BEST MASTER TRAITS:

Can learn

Can use tools

Brave (sometimes too brave)

EVIL RATING: 8 out of 10 skulls

FAVOURITE MEMORIES:

How the Minions lost the Caveman as their master:

It turns out that if you equip your master with a fly swatter to fight a bear, what you'll learn about your master is that the bear usually wins.

CAVE PAINTINGS

Caveman loved to decorate his cave with paintings. Can you doodle cave paintings all over this page?

SPOT THE DIFFERENCE

During Cro-Minion times, you always had to keep a sharp eye out for danger. Look at these two images. Can you spot ten differences between them?

HOW DID YOU DO?
Check your answers
on page 94.

ANCIENT EGYPT FACT FILE

MASTER: ANCIENT EGYPTIANS

The Ancient Egyptians were full of promise. They were smart and they loved to build massive monuments. So what could go wrong . . . ?

FACT FILE

NAME: Ancient Egyptians

TIME PERIOD: 5,000 years ago

BEST MASTER TRAITS:

Awesome builders

Pharaohs think they're gods

Cool outfits

EVIL RATING: 7 out of 10 skulls

FAVOURITE MEMORIES:

How the Minions lost the Ancient Egyptians as their master:

Note to all Minions: always, always ensure that blueprints are the correct way up.

BROKEN VASE

The Ancient Egyptians loved a good vase. Unfortunately, delicate pottery plus Minions always ends up with something being broken. Can you match the correct broken pieces back to where they belong and then reconstruct the vase on the next page?

1

2

3

4

5

6 **7** **8** **9** **10**

ANCIENT EGYPTIAN BLUEPRINT

The Pharaoh wants a new monument built – the biggest and best ever. Sketch out a design for a monument below. Don't forget to keep your blueprint the right way up.

PIRATE ERA
FACT FILE

MASTER: PIRATES

Sailing the seven seas, plundering treasure and singing cool songs – the Minions were very happy to serve their pirate master.

Fact file

NAME: Pirates

TIME PERIOD: 400 years ago

BEST MASTER TRAITS:

Great hats

Life at sea

Lots of jobs to do on deck

EVIL RATING: 5 out of 10 skulls

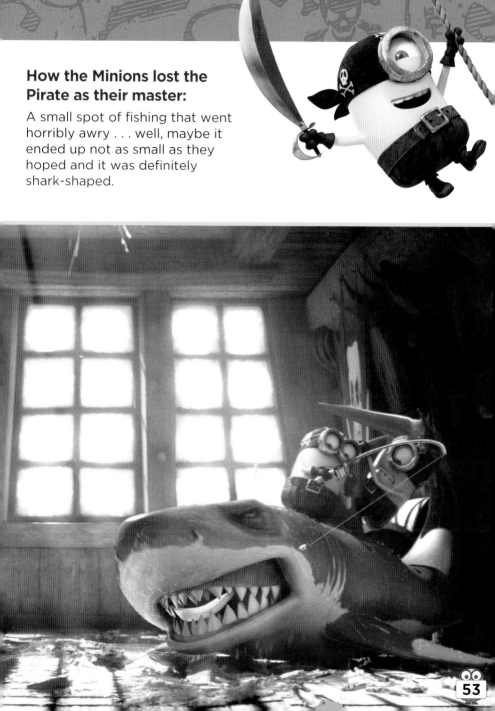

How the Minions lost the Pirate as their master:

A small spot of fishing that went horribly awry . . . well, maybe it ended up not as small as they hoped and it was definitely shark-shaped.

FOLLOW THAT FISHING LINE

Arrrgh, m'hearties! The Minions have caught something on their fishing line – what is it?

Follow the line from the pirate Minions to find out.

HOW DID YOU DO? Check your answers on page 94.

PIRATE PHRASES

One of the best things about having a pirate master is that you get to speak like a pirate.

How many words can you make out of these arrrghh-some phrases?

"SHIVER ME TIMBERS"

_____

_____

_____

"WALK THE PLANK"

_____

_____

_____

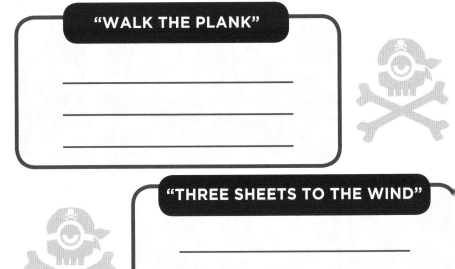

"THREE SHEETS TO THE WIND"

_____

_____

_____

Now, using all letters combined in all phrases, see what other words you can create!

_____

_____

_____

_____

_____

_____

_____

VIVE LE MINION
FACT FILE

MASTER: NAPOLEON

There were lots of great things about Napoleon; he was smart, a savvy commander and he loved conquering things. But then, it all went . . . BOOM!

FACT FILE

NAME: Napoleon Bonaparte

TIME PERIOD: 200 years ago

BEST MASTER TRAITS:

Good eye contact

Massive army

Big plans to invade other countries

EVIL RATING: 9 out of 10 skulls

How the Minions lost Napoleon Bonaparte as their master:

If you're short and want to get a better view of things, it's best to climb onto something. However, that *something* should never be a cannon behind your master . . .

LET'S PLAY
SQUARES

Battles are fun, mostly, but there's a lot of waiting around. Luckily the Minions knew about this game to pass the time.

How to play:

- Take turns drawing a line between any two side-by-side dots. The player who draws the fourth line that makes a square, conquers that square, marks it with their initials, then takes another turn.

- Once all the squares that can be made have been completed, the player with the most squares marked with their initials WINS and is called the "Mighty Minion In Charge" for the rest of the day!

BOOM – UH, OH!

The French army did not take kindly to the accidental 'loss' of Napoleon and chased the Minions all the way to the icy wasteland of the polar ice cap.

Can you guide the Minions through the maze to their ice cave sanctuary?

→ START

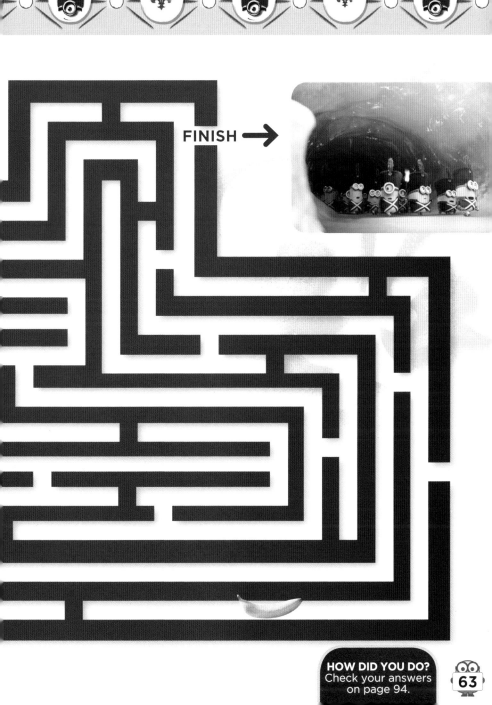

FINISH →

ICE CAVE FACT FILE

The Minions found a safe home in an ice cave. It was the dawn of the Minions' very own civilisation.

When they first found th cave, the Minions were excited. They built snow houses, ate snow cones, snowball fights and ever started their very own cl

But without a master, the Minions soon lost all purpose and became bored. If they didn't find a master, and soon, they would perish.

Until one day, a Minion called Kevin came up with a plan to find them a new master. But he needed help. He got it from from Stuart (who was asleep and had no idea what he was volunteering for) and Bob (because of his enthusiasm but mainly because of the lack of other volunteers).

OFF THEY WENT,
IN SEARCH OF A NEW MASTER!

ICE SPY

The long winter days don't fly by in the Minions' ice cave.

Can you spot 10 differences between these pictures? It should help to pass the time.

JOKE:

Why can't you say a joke while standing on ice?

Because it might crack up!

 **HOW DID YOU DO?** Check your answers on page 95.

 67

VILLAIN-CON
FACT FILE

There's so much to do, it's criminal:

- **ATTEND GUEST LECTURES FROM ESTEEMED VILLAINS.**

- **MAKE CONTACTS IN THE UNDERWORLD COMMUNITY.**

- **LEARN YOUR CRIMINAL TRADE.**

- **SAMPLE THE NEWEST IN VILLAIN TECHNOLOGY.**

- **MEET YOUR IDOLS AND EVEN FIND YOUR DREAM JOB.**

- And for the first time **ANYWHERE** a special appearance from the first female super villain, **SCARLET OVERKILL!**

DO YOU HAVE WHAT IT TAKES?

FIND OUT!

Industry professionals will be on-hand throughout the convention to offer critique and review your villainous skills.

ASK A PROFESSIONAL TO HELP YOU ON THE NEXT STEP OF YOUR CRIMINAL CAREER!

IT'S THAT TIME OF YEAR AGAIN

VILLAIN-CON INTERNATIONAL

HITCHHIKING TO VILLAIN-CON

Help Kevin, Stuart and Bob get to Villain-Con.
Decode the address for Villain-Con using the
alphabet decoder.

A	B	C	D	E	F	G	H	I	J	K	L

M	N	O	P	Q	R	S	T	U	V	W	X

Y	Z	0	1	2	3	4	5	6	7	8	9

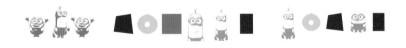

___ ___ ___ ___ ___ ___ ___ ___ ___ ___ ___ ___

___ ___ ___ ___ ___ ___ ___ ___ ___ ___ ___

___ ___ ___ ___ ___ ___

Now you know the address, help our hero trio fill in their sign so they can hitchhike!

HOW DID YOU DO?
Check your answers on page 95.

SCARLET OVERKILL
FACT FILE

Move aside, men. There's a new bad man in town and that man is a woman.

FACT FILE

NAME: Scarlet Overkill

APPEARANCE: Impeccably stylish! 1960s beehive hairdo, red dress, long black gloves

LOVES: Rubies, Herb, her trophies of crime, the English Royal Family (especially their jewels!)

HATES: When her henchmen fail and betray her.

MOST EVIL MOMENT: Overthrowing the English throne.

MOST LIKELY TO SAY:

"DOESN'T IT FEEL SO GOOD TO BE BAD?"

HERB OVERKILL
FACT FILE

He's a super-genius inventor and the husband of Scarlet Overkill. He's cool, he's hip and he's crazy (in love with Scarlet)!

FACT FILE

NAME: Herb Overkill

APPEARANCE: Cool hair, cool suit, he's simply just cool.

LOVES: Scarlet, inventing, gadgets, soup, romance, explosions.

FUNNIEST/MOST EVIL MOMENT: Taking selfies with vintage torture devices.

MOST LIKELY TO SAY:

"IT WAS ME, HERB, THE WHOLE TIME!"

"IT'S UNBELIEVABLE, **BUT** BELIEVE IT!"

Scarlet Overkill has received a mushy, gushy love letter (ewww!).

Can you solve the clues and find the true identity of her secret admirer?

You will always be my queen

*Love,
your secret admirer*

xXx

CLUES:

1. **HE'S A COOL CAT AND A SUPER-GENIUS INVENTOR**

2. **HE HAS AN AWESOME SECRET LAB WHERE HE INVENTS EVIL GADGETS**

3. **HE'S AN OLD ROMANTIC AT HEART**

4. **HE WEARS A SHARP, BLUE SUIT**

Scarlet's secret
admirer is:

_____

_____

HOW DID YOU DO?
Check your answers
on page 95.

MAKE A SPLASH AT
VILLAIN-CON

Villain-Con is an exciting place – but if you're not careful, you'll get too overwhelmed and miss all the BEST stuff.

Plan your day at Villain-Con below.

_____

_____

_____

_____

_____

_____

_____

_____

_____

_____

_____

_____

_____

WELCOME TO
VILLAIN-CON 1968

For 89 years the biggest
gathering of criminals fro
around the globe.

Brought to you by the Vill.
Network Channel –
**"If you tell anyone,
we'll find you!"**

545 Oran
Grove
Avenu
Orland
Florid

INTERNATIONAL
VILLAIN
CONVENTION

DO YOU HAVE WHAT IT TAKE
FIND OUT!

Industry professionals will be
on-hand throughout the
convention to offer critique
and review your villainous skills.
Ask a professional to help you
on the next step of your
criminal career!

Pretze
Delicio
Warm Pre

Even villa
need to ea
find us n
to the Pa
Room B

ere's so much to do, it's criminal:

...end guest lectures from esteemed villains.

...ke contacts in the underworld community.

...rn your criminal trade.

...mple the newest in villain technology.

...et your idols and even find your dream job.

...d for the first time ANYWHERE a special

...pearance from the first female super villain,

...ARLET OVERKILL!

...tional Villain-Con Exclusives:

...e Cracking Booth

...us and find the best way to get into that

... quickly and without fuss.

...s easy as click, click, open!

...chmen Placement Specialist

...'ve been helping place the industry's best

...hmen for more than 60 years. Even if you're a

...d – we'll find you that dream job!

...eze Ray Booth

...efario will show you how to be a cool criminal

...his newest gadget, the FREEZE RAY!

... Rick

... your very own copy of Sick Rick's How

...e a bad guy in 10 days.

Villain-Con – so much fun, it's a crime!

NO PHOTOS ALLOWED.

If you would like your photograph

taken with your criminal idol,

please purchase one from an

official Villain-Con photographer.

DESIGN YOUR OWN
MINION ARMY

Every super villain needs a Minion army. Have you ever imagined having your own? Even just a little bit . . . of course you have!

Well, they'll need a uniform, Minions **LOVE** awesome outfits. Design them below.

Here are some previous uniform examples:

THROW A MINIONS PARTY!

The Minions know how to have a party! Here's how you can, too!

DECORATIONS

- **MAKE EVERYTHING YELLOW** with a touch of blue, of course!
- **BUY SOME WOBBLY EYES** from a craft shop and stick them onto your guests' cups.

FOOD AND DRINK

- BANANA CAKE
- BANANAS
- PINEAPPLE JUICE (IT'S YELLOW!)
- CUPCAKES

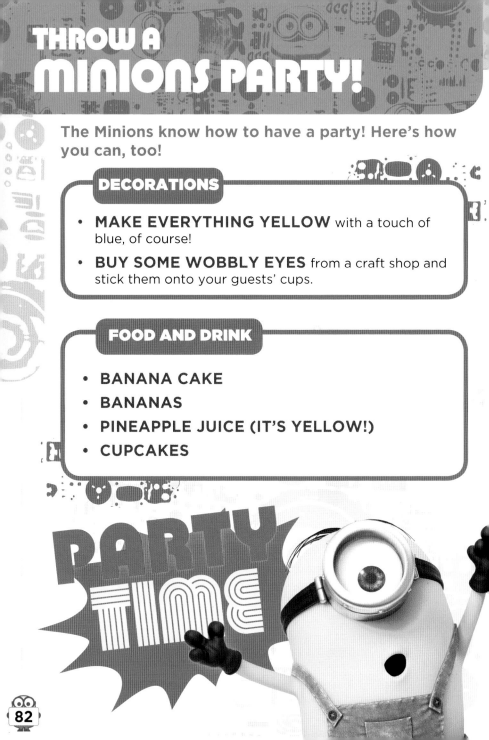

PARTY TIME

PIN THE GOGGLES ON THE MINION

- On a large piece of paper, draw a Minion but without his goggles. Colour him in yellow. On a separate piece of paper, draw some Minion goggles and colour them in. Ask an adult to help you cut them out.

- Put some sticky putty on the back of the goggles. Each player should be blind-folded and spun around five times. Then they should try to stick the goggles as closely as they can to the correct position. The person whose goggles are closest, wins!

MAKE EACH OF YOUR GUESTS THEIR VERY OWN SET OF MINION GOGGLES FROM CARD!

PARTY

BANANA FACT FILE

They're the fruit the Minions love, but how much do you know about that delicious yellow fruit?

Read on and swot up!

- **Bananas have been growing on Earth for over 1 million years** *(nearly as long as the Minions have been on Earth!)*

- **Bananas don't grow on trees, they grown on giant herbs** *(the plant herb, not Herb Overkill!)*

- **Bunches of bananas grow pointing upwards – how weird is that?**

- **Historians think it was likely that bananas were the first fruit to be farmed by humans** *(I wonder whose idea that was...!)*

- **Bananas are berries. Yes, it's true, but prepare to have your mind blown even wider – strawberries are not berries.**

- **Bananas are slightly radioactive, making them the perfect, evil fruit!** *(Only very slightly – eating them won't turn you into a super hero, unfortunately.)*

- **Eating bananas that contain lots of good stuff will cheer you up – it's the secret to why the Minions are always so happy!**

- **A bunch of bananas is called a hand; an individual banana is a finger.**

MY FAVOURITE THINGS

Scribble down your favourite things as fast as you can to discover what you're really thinking!

COLOUR

NUMBER

ANIMAL

SEASON

HOBBY

BEST FRIEND

SONG

BOOK

SMELL

DRINK

FOOD

MUSIC GROUP

FLOWER

GAME

MINION

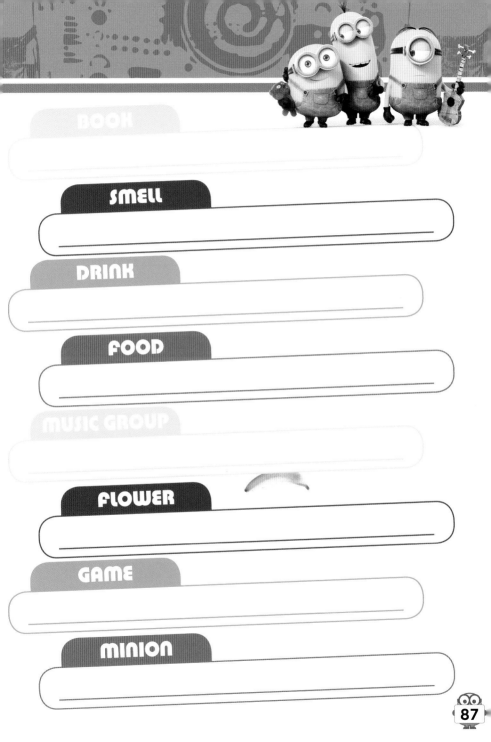

MY BIGGEST SECRETS

Everyone has secrets. Small secrets, big secrets, good secrets, evil secrets.

Fill in your most secret-est secrets onto these pages and then place invisible tape along the edge of the page so no one will ever notice your hidden pages.

MY BIGGEST SECRET IS:

_____

_____

_____

_____

MY SECRET DREAM IS:

_____

_____

_____

_____

_____

ONE THING I SECRETLY LIKE IS:

_____

_____

_____

_____

_____

MY SECRET DREAM FOR THE FUTURE IS:

_____

_____

_____

_____

_____

I TRUST THIS PERSON WITH ALL MY SECRETS:

_____

MY DIARY

Use these pages to write about the adventures of your day. There's no event or adventure too big or too small, so let's get creative!

MY DIARY

PAGE 23
There are 30 Minions
There are 10 Minions with one eye

PAGE 44-45

PAGE 36-37

PAGE 48-49

7
1
8
5
6
4

PAGE 62-63

FINISH →

→ START

PAGE 54-55

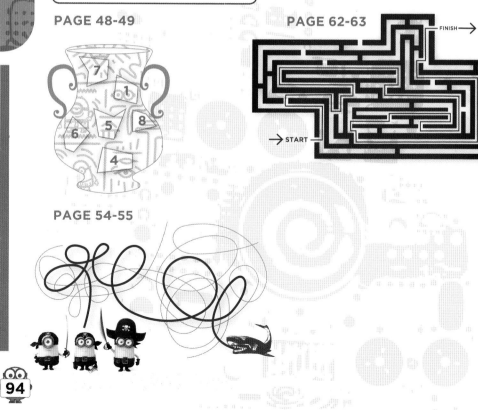